In the Hands
of the Enemy

by Robert Sheely

Illustrated by John F. Martin

SILVER MOON PRESS
NEW YORK

For information:
Silver Moon Press
New York, NY
(800) 874–3320

Library of Congress Cataloging-in-Publication Data

Sheely, Robert, 1956-
    In the hands of the enemy / by Robert Sheely ; illustrated by John F. Martin ; [edited by
Hope L. Killcoyne].-- 1st Silver Moon Press ed.
    p. cm. -- (Adventures in America ; 8)
    Summary: Lost in the woods near Plymouth Colony, fourteen-year-old John, a member of
the trouble-making Billington family that accompanied the Pilgrims on their Mayflower
voyage in 1620, receives shelter and nourishment from the Nauset tribe.
    ISBN 1-893110-31-1
    [1. Lost children--Fiction. 2. Nauset Indians--Fiction. 3. Indians of North
America--Massachusetts--Fiction. 4. Plymouth (Mass.)--History--17th century--Fiction.] I.
Martin, John F., ill. II. Killcoyne, Hope L. III. Title. IV. Series

PZ7.S5405In 2003
[Fic]--dc21
                                                                                    2002044563

10   9   8   7   6   5   4   3   2   1
Printed in the USA

For Annette, the best ally and supporter
any writer could ask for.
Also big thanks to Hope and David
for their invaluable guidance
throughout this project.

Thanks,
Rob

ONE

LOST

FOURTEEN-YEAR-OLD JOHN BILLINGTON, Jr., was lost. He did not want to admit it to himself at first. Just over the next hill he was sure to find something familiar, something to lead him back to Plymouth Colony. So again and again he climbed the next hill—only to find nothing familiar at all.

He was definitely lost.

The sun was getting dangerously low in the sky as John stood still for a moment, forcing himself not to swat at the mosquitoes that were constantly swarming around him and biting his hands, his arms, his face. He listened for the cries of the search party that was sure to be sent out for him. But he heard nothing—except for the buzzing of the mosquitoes.

He did not dare yell or cry out himself. These woods contained savages who might very well kill an English boy if they found him wandering alone. There were also wolves and other wild creatures who would like nothing better than to feast on that same English boy's bones. John swatted at the tormenting insects and forced himself not to think about these things. He said yet another prayer for a quick rescue and a safe journey home.

But just in case, he needed to find some place to hide for the night.

* * *

The moon was waxing toward fullness but only beyond the cover of the trees. Beneath the thick canopy of foliage, the night was as black as pitch. John knew just how black that was because he had seen the *Mayflower's* crew use a black tarry substance they called "pitch" to seal cracks in the hull of the ship, preparing it for the upcoming voyage. John held his hands in front of his face. He couldn't even see them.

He curled up in a hollow at the base of a big oak tree. He had dragged some small branches to make a bed and some larger ones to put around to hide him from enemies—human or otherwise. Some said the wolves were demons, creatures of the devil himself. John knew he should trust in the Lord to protect him from demons, and he had said his prayers more than once this night, but still he could not sleep.

How could he have been so stupid as to get lost in the woods? The shame of it! As if he did not feel enough already. The main source of young John's shame was his family. The Billingtons had come across to America on the *Mayflower* with the Separatists, those Puritans who had split from the Church of England. But the Billingtons were not members of the church. There were not enough church families to fill up the *Mayflower*, so the

Puritans asked some other English families, such as the Billingtons, to come along with them. The church members called these people *Strangers*. In return the Strangers called the church members *Saints*.

From the very beginning young John had felt the sting of being a Stranger. The rest of his family had not made it any easier for him. His father, John, Sr., was an outspoken critic of the Saints. John burned with embarrassment as his father argued with the church leaders and even questioned the authority of Captain Miles Standish, the military leader of Plymouth Colony.

In fact, after landing at Plymouth, John's father had openly disobeyed an order from the Captain. He was brought before the elders of the community. After listening to the evidence, they pronounced him guilty and decided his punishment: "You are sentenced to have your feet tied to your neck for one day."

Mr. Billington turned pale and fell to his knees in front of the elders. "Please, sirs. I humbly beg your pardon. Have mercy on me."

"Very well," said Captain Standish and the other members of the community. "We will show you mercy this time. But do not try our patience again."

John's face burned at the very memory of that incident. But it wasn't the first humiliating scene involving a Billington. Back on the *Mayflower*, John's younger brother Francis had found some gunpowder in their father's cabin and decided to play with it. He had wrapped a little of the gunpowder in a piece of paper and set it on fire. The resulting explosion almost set the entire ship on fire. Much head-shaking followed this episode. "Those Billingtons!" whispered the colonists. John wanted to die.

And now, as if things were not bad enough, he, John Billington, Jr., had to go and get himself lost in the woods like a helpless child. Between his memories of disgrace and his fears for his own life, John did not sleep at all the entire night. He no longer felt certain that help would come from Plymouth. If he were to get out of this, he'd have to help himself.

* * *

The next day, John tried using the rising sun to determine which direction was east. He then tried to head toward the north and east, because that was probably where Plymouth was. But by afternoon the sky filled with clouds, hiding the sun. John kept moving in what he hoped was the right direction, but it was impossible to move in a straight line. There were too many thornbushes, dense undergrowth, and trees.

Some of the thornbushes held berries, and John ate all the ones he could reach. It helped take the edge off his hunger, but his stomach still growled, and he could not stop thinking about his mother's cooking and how satisfying it would be to enjoy some of it right then.

In a clearing, John spied a small heap of dirt that looked as if it had been made by human hands. John fell to his knees and began digging. Captain

Standish and some of the other settlers had told stories of finding heaps of dirt just like this on their first explorations of the American mainland. In those heaps the search party had found baskets of corn buried by the natives. The colonists had gathered up as much of the corn as they could carry and brought it back to the ship.

John dug and dug, but he found no corn nor anything else edible in this particular heap—just dirt.

Every so often he would stumble upon a small creek and kneel down to drink his fill. Mostly, he just kept moving, always hoping to find something familiar over the next hill.

He crested one hill and surprised a herd of deer. They scattered at his approach, and John dropped to the ground, as startled by the deer as they were by him. In an instant, the deer fled, and once again, he was all alone in the forest.

Eventually, evening fell and it was time to make another shelter. As before, John found himself a large tree and cleared out a hollow at its base. He collected branches to make a bed and to hide him from all enemies. He said his prayers, asking God to forgive his family's transgressions, and send someone strong and brave. He asked God to soften Captain Standish's heart enough to rescue him.

This night he slept, but only for a little bit at a time. Again and again, a noise would awaken him, and he would lie absolutely still, listening for the footstep of a native or the growl of a wolf. When the night would grow quiet again, John would fall back to fitful sleep, his dreams filled with memories of dishonor, visions of danger.

*   *   *

Soon the days began to run together in John's mind. Hunger and lack of sleep left him weak and increasingly unable to think clearly. An afternoon thunderstorm soaked him to the bone; he spent the following night shivering and shaking.

The next day, though the sun came out and warmed the air, John could not seem to get warm himself. He walked along, shivering and talking to himself. Sometimes he thought he heard voices calling his name, but every time he would stop and listen, the voices disappeared. His clothes had become crusted with dirt and torn from the many thorns and brambles. His skin, too, was scratched and cut, and the mosquitoes tormented him unmercifully.

Finally, he became too tired to walk and he just sat down at the base of a tree. There was a hollow in a nearby rock that held an inch or so of dirty water. John scooped the water up in his hands and drank it. It tasted bad, but he was so thirsty that he did not care.

John leaned his head back against the tree and stared out at the forest in front of him. Figures began to appear before his eyes. A party of settlers led by Captain Standish. John almost cried out for joy, but some part of his mind realized that the figures were not real. He was seeing things, like a dream but with his eyes wide open. After a moment, he recognized the scene playing out before him. It was a story he had heard many times in the last few months. The settlers even had a name for it; they called it "The First Encounter."

It happened to Captain Standish's exploration party the night after they had discovered the mounds of buried corn. John could see the men now in his strange waking dream, making a fire, posting a guard, and settling down to sleep for the night. Then he saw other figures slowly sneak up on the sleeping settlers, undetected by the guard.

These figures were wrapped in animal skins, carrying bows and arrows. They hid behind trees and encircled the colonists' camp. Then, when the sun was just rising, the Indians attacked. They screamed and fired arrows into the camp.

John's heart beat in his chest as he watched this scene unfold in front of him. He felt a surge of pride as he saw Captain Standish grab his musket and begin firing back at the attackers. The other Englishmen grabbed their guns and fired, too. Amazingly, no one on either side was hit by either arrow or bullet. But one of Captain Standish's shots hit a tree inches from the leader of the attacking Indians, a tall, fierce-looking figure, whose name they would learn was Aspinet. Aspinet spun, moving back, calling to his men to retreat.

The Indians slipped away as the colonists continued firing. Captain Standish summoned a few of his men and tried to pursue the retreating figures, but they had vanished.

John smiled at the figure of Captain Standish standing in front of him, strong and brave and ready to kill an enemy. Then, as the strange vision slipped away from John's eyes, he saw that there was indeed a figure standing in front of him. He blinked to clear his eyes, then looked up again.

There standing in front of John, clear as day, was a native, dressed in animal skins, a single feather dangling from his long dark hair. In his hands were a bow and an arrow, pointed right at John Billington's heart.

TWO

ALONE

A MANUITT WAS NOT LOST. HE HAD SPENT A large part of his fourteen years in these woods. He knew the trails like old friends. He had been hunting here since he was a little boy, barely old enough to carry a bow and tag along with the older boys.

Today he was practicing his hunting skills with his cousin Potak. It had been a while since Amanuitt had seen him, but somehow he felt like being alone today. He quickened his pace and struck out on his own, leaving his cousin behind.

Amanuitt could read the forest. Almost everything it contained had something to say to him. The paw print in the dried mud beside a stream told Amanuitt that a gray wolf—a large male by the size of the print—had passed this way recently. Broken twigs and nibbled bark spoke of a herd of deer; perhaps the wolf had been following them. Or perhaps he was after the rabbit whose tooth marks were visible on some torn blades of grass at the base of a skinny elm.

Amanuitt saw all these signs, but they barely registered. His mind was preoccupied with other thoughts. Thoughts of anger and hatred.

Amanuitt was a Nauset. The Nausets were a small tribe that lived across the bay from Plymouth on a hook of land that the English called Cape Cod. They belonged to the larger community of Wampanoag or *People of the Dawn*. Mostly, the Wampanoag thought of themselves simply as the *People*.

The People had lived on this land for thousands of years. They were hunters, farmers, and fishers. They had both winter villages and summer villages. The winter villages were inland where the People would be sheltered from the harsh weather. The summer villages were along the coast where they fished and cultivated crops.

The leaders of the People were called Sachems. The Sachem of the Nausets was Aspinet. Like the Sachems of the other Wampanoag tribes, Aspinet ruled not by power and fear, but by persuasion. The Nausets followed him because they were convinced of his knowledge and wisdom.

Things had been this way for as long as any of the People could remember, certainly for as long as Amanuitt could recall. The People were proud of their traditions. Their ways had provided for them for many generations. And life was good for the People.

But all that had changed with the coming of the strange ships from across the ocean.

The English were not the first white men to reach the land of the People. There had been other visitors, ships bearing strange men who called themselves Spaniards, and still others who called themselves Frenchmen.

The People had learned to treat these pale-skinned men with caution. Sometimes the strangers would act like civilized men and offer their hands in friendship. Other times, the strangers would attack for no apparent reason.

Six years before the arrival of the *Mayflower*, another party of English ships had come! They were led by a man named Captain John Smith. The People watched him carefully. They soon saw that he had come in peace. The People offered him hospitality.

Later that year Captain Smith sailed back to England, but he left a ship behind in the charge of a man named Thomas Hunt. The People extended him the same courtesy they had shown Captain Smith.

Thomas Hunt appeared to be grateful for the People's hospitality. One day, he invited 20 young Patuxet and seven Nauset men on board his ship. But when these men ventured on board, Hunt and his men grabbed them, wrapped them in chains, and stole them away.

Their friends and families could only watch in horror from the shore as the great ship sailed off with their loved ones inside. Among the kidnapped young men was a Nauset warrior by the name of Epenow. And among those watching helplessly onshore was Epenow's young brother, a five-year-old boy named Amanuitt.

And as if that were not enough of a tragedy, a Great Sickness soon swept across the People. Thousands of them grew sick and died. Whole villages were wiped out completely, leaving not a single living soul behind.

The Nausets were hit hard by the Sickness. Two-thirds of them were killed, leaving barely 500 Nausets alive. Amanuitt's mother and father died, leaving him without a family. That just served to make Amanuitt long even more for the brother who had been stolen away—and to hate the evil English who had taken him.

*   *   *

Amanuitt was so distracted by his own thoughts that he almost didn't notice the broken branch by the side of the trail. It was of medium size, hanging at about shoulder height off the ground—too high to be a deer's grazing. Besides, the branch was dead with no tender leaves or fresh bark to tempt the appetite of a deer.

It was possible a clumsy bear had brushed against the branch and snapped it, but that didn't seem likely. Then Amanuitt noticed the tracks at the base of the tree with the broken branch. These tracks were strange: large and unlike any Amanuitt had ever seen before.

These were not made by any animal. They could only be of human origin. But what kind of moccasins were shaped like this? And look how strangely the different prints were spaced. Who would travel through the forest so awkwardly? Who would take so little care to cover his tracks?

Could this be a trap set by the Naragansetts, the

historic enemies of the People? Had they invaded Wampanoag land and placed these strange tracks here to lure an unsuspecting member of the People?

No, it didn't make any sense. But if not Wampanoag or Naragansett, then who could have made these tracks? As soon as he asked himself the question, the answer struck Amanuitt like a bolt of lightning from the sky.

It could only be the English.

Every nerve in Amanuitt's body awakened. He knew he should go back and find his cousin. He had no business tracking the English by himself. He was one, alone. This might well be only one set of footprints from a much larger English party. And with only 14 years, he was not yet an adult, not yet a full warrior.

But Amanuitt did not listen to his wiser self. Instead he followed the tracks. It was not hard. Amanuitt did not need to use any of the tracking skills he had learned first from his beloved brother Epenow, and then from the other men of the Nauset community, after Epenow had been kidnapped.

Amanuitt came to a patch of berry vines. He bent down to study them. The vines were torn and stripped almost clean. There was also a bright patch of color at the end of one vine. Amanuitt pulled the vine closer and discovered a small piece of cloth snagged on one of the thorns. He took the cloth in his hands and studied it. It was unlike anything he had ever held before. The color was a rich blue and the fabric felt thick and smooth in his fingers.

"English," Amanuitt thought to himself.

*   *   *

Even though Amanuitt did not admit it to himself, there was a simple reason he did not want to find his cousin and tell him of his discovery—a reason why he wanted to keep this particular hunt to himself. Barely a few months earlier, Massasoit, the Sachem of the Pokanoket, had startled everyone by making peace with the English.

Amanuitt could not believe the news. How could the People make peace with these terrible intruders whose countrymen had stolen away his beloved brother?

The answer had come at a meeting of the entire Nauset community. Aspinet in his role as the Nauset Sachem explained why he supported Massasoit's decision to make peace with the former enemy, and why he thought the rest of the Nausets should support it as well.

"These are not the same Englishmen who betrayed our friendship before," Aspinet had said. "They have brought their families with them. They have built a village. Are these the activities of people who come in war?"

"But did these new English not steal our sacred corn?" asked a member of the community. "The corn we placed in the ground for the spirits of our dead?"

"That is true," said Aspinet. "And I was as angered as you when I saw this. I led a party to attack them for their theft. However, Massasoit has sent word that the English have apologized for the taking of our corn. Their customs are not the same as ours. They did not know what they were doing."

"That may be so, but what does it gain us to give them our trust?" asked another Nauset.

"These are difficult times for the People," answered Aspinet. "The Great Sickness has taken many of our strong and brave warriors. We are no longer able to defend ourselves against the Naragansett who were spared the Great Sickness. We need an ally to stand beside us should the Naragansett decide to attack."

The rest of the Nausets reluctantly acknowledged the wisdom of Aspinet's words. They agreed to consider making a peace treaty of their own with the English.

* * *

Amanuitt moved more quickly now, careful not to make any noise that would alert his quarry. He followed the tracks over hills and through valleys, growing ever closer to his target. He felt the blood beat in his ears, pounding like the drums of war.

He could not stop himself; all he wanted was to hurt the English as he had been hurt, to make the English feel the same pain he had, to ease his own hurt with the comfort of revenge.

Amanuitt rounded a slight bend in the trail, and there he was. An Englishman sprawled against the base of a large tree, staring into space. Amanuitt froze for a moment as the Englishman's face turned to look into his. Amanuitt saw that it was just a boy, no older than Amanuitt himself. A look of puzzlement crossed the English boy's face as if he were trying to decide if Amanuitt were real or some kind of ghost.

"May the spirit of my brother Epenow make my hand steady and my aim true," said Amanuitt. He lifted his bow and stepped forward.

THREE

CAPTURED

JOHN STARED AT THE FIGURE IN FRONT OF him with its arrow poised to strike. He could see the tip of the arrow very clearly. It seemed to be made of some kind of sharpened rock. John's eyes focused intently on the tip, frozen in front of him.

Suddenly a wave of sadness washed over John at the thought that he would die like this, so far from home. He wished he had been a better person, a better son, a better brother, a better friend. Now he would never get the chance.

Something caught John's eye. A flash of movement in the trees behind the figure with the bow and arrow. John turned his eyes toward the movement just as a hand reached out from the trees and grabbed the arm holding the bow.

The native boy whirled around to find another, taller, native boy. The first barked out a few angry syllables in a language very strange to John's ears. The other boy answered back in a calmer voice.

Back and forth the two went, the bow clutched between them. John followed them with his eyes until suddenly he was too tired to keep his eyes open at all. Exhaustion washed over him, and he felt himself sinking into blackness.

*   *   *

When John awoke, the world was upside down. He looked down at the sky. It was moving, along with a series of upside-down trees that swam through his field of vision. "How strange," he thought. "Am I dead? Is this heaven?"

Then John gradually became aware of a pair of arms wrapped around his legs, something strong and solid pressing into his stomach. By the time he came to his senses enough to realize that he was being carried over someone's shoulder, whoever had hoisted him up there stopped and set him down on the ground, helping him lean back against a large boulder.

John looked up at him, expecting to find the face he'd seen before, behind the bow and arrow. But this was the other native boy, the one who had saved his life. A voice spoke off to John's left, and he turned to find the first boy, now holding two bows. He spoke to the one who had been carrying John, then gestured in John's direction.

The taller, and John could see, older boy responded. John listened as both of them spoke in their strange tongue. He looked them over. Both had long, dark hair with one large feather hanging down in the back. Both were barefoot. Each was dressed in a leather breechcloth with a belt of woven leather. From each belt hung a pouch that looked to be made of soft deerskin. The taller one wore a necklace strung with shells and small pieces of bone. The other, the one who had almost killed him, had a knife in a leather sheath hanging from a cord around his neck.

His would-be killer set down the bows and came over to crouch in front of John. Reaching into a leather pouch on his belt, his knife dangling, the boy pulled out a handful of some kind of cooked grain and held it out to John. John stared at the grain, suspicious of the boy's intention.

Impatiently, the boy gestured for John to take the grain. When John still hesitated, the boy took John's hands and poured the grain into them. The boy stood up, muttering a few words. The other one said something, then let go a small laugh.

John stared at the strange grain in his hands. What was it? Was it safe to eat? Well, John admitted to himself, if the young Indian had not killed him earlier, it did not seem likely he would try to poison him now. John lifted some grain to his lips and chewed it tentatively. It was nutty tasting and crunchy. John swallowed. The moment after he decided it tasted good, he thought he was going to be sick. His stomach had had little food for days, and it seemed unwilling to accept anything new. But the sick feeling passed, and John ate the rest of the grain without becoming ill.

Feeling stronger, he tried to stand. But five days without real food and only dirty water had taken its toll. His head swam and his legs crumpled beneath him and he collapsed back against the boulder. The two young natives watched John, then spoke a few words to one another. Then the taller one walked over to the two bows lying on the ground and picked them up. The shorter boy, the one whose face was now burned forever into John's memory, walked up to John, bent down, and hoisted him up over his shoulder like a sack of grain.

Without another word, they headed off down the trail.

*   *   *

They stopped a short while later by a stream. The two native boys knelt and drank. John, his mouth as dry as he could ever remember it being, drank, too. The water was cool and clear. Again and again, John dipped his hands into the stream and lifted them to his lips, feeling his body take in the water like a sponge.

The boys shared some more of their grain. John ate it eagerly, even holding out his hands for more. He was feeling much better now. His body was stronger and his head clearer. He began to think about his situation. The boys had not killed him. They seemed to be escorting him out of the woods and back to Plymouth. The peace treaty between his people and the natives must be working. Signed months earlier, it appeared to be saving his life. He shuddered to think what these two might have done to him had a treaty not been signed.

If these young natives were peaceful, he reasoned,

then perhaps they might have learned some words of English. He decided to try them.

"Hello," he said. There was no response. "My name is John. What is yours?" The boys just looked at him. "I am English." That seemed to get a reaction. "English." Yes, they knew that word. They looked at each other and then back at him. "I live at Plymouth Colony." No reaction this time. "Plymouth. That is where we are headed."

The boys turned to each other again and spoke a few words in their language. They gestured for John to stand. John stood, still shaky on his feet, but feeling much better than before. He took a few steps. His legs grew steadier with each step. The shorter boy gave a grunt and started off down the trail. John followed, and the taller boy brought up the rear.

The pace at first was more than John could manage. The boy behind him called out to the one in front and they all slowed down. John found himself staring at the bare feet of the boy in front of him. How could he walk like that through the woods? How could he step on stones and through thornbushes? John's feet were in pretty bad shape themselves. His shoes were firm enough to protect him from stones and thorns, but they were hand-me-downs from another boy who had outgrown them. They were tight in front and pinched his toes, and in back they were loose and rubbed blisters on John's heels and ankles.

John limped along, happy at last to be on his way home. Then the boys came to a clearing and John

looked up at the late afternoon sun. It was on his right.

On his right.

That meant west was on his right. And straight ahead, the direction they were travelling, was south.

South.

Away from Plymouth Colony.

*   *   *

John tried not to let the boys see that he knew they were heading away from Plymouth. He kept moving, his face outwardly calm. Behind that face, his mind raced.

Where were they taking him? Did they plan to harm him? Or perhaps their intention was to hold him for ransom. He almost laughed at the thought. After all the troubles his family had caused, the leaders of Plymouth would hardly be eager to pay ransom for a Billington. They would more likely offer to pay the Indians to keep him.

John followed along, glancing up into the sky whenever they left the trees and passed out into the open. They had turned now and were headed east. Still away from Plymouth. And toward who knew what?

He studied the boy in front of him whenever he could. He was strong, obviously. His arms and legs were muscled, and he moved easily through the forest. And he was armed with a bow, arrows, and a knife. Not to mention the taller and probably stronger boy behind him with his own weapons.

Then John remembered. He was armed, too. He had a folding knife. He forced himself not to reach into his pocket to check for it. He walked along steadily, his heart pounding in his ears until the two boys stopped to confer with each other. John slipped his hand into his pocket and, yes, there was the folding knife.

John slid his hand back out again, suddenly calmer about his situation. His knife was small, and he would have to open it before it could be used as a weapon. This would make it harder to catch his captors by surprise, but still, he did have a weapon. And something else, too.

The knife was more than a weapon for John. It was a symbol. It had been given to him as a gift by Samuel, his best friend among the other boys. Samuel was a Saint, too—perhaps the only Saint who didn't hold John in low esteem because he was a Stranger. Samuel and John had become friends during the long voyage. On days when the sea was particularly rough, the boys would distract and calm each other by talking about all the fun things they were going to do once they landed in the New World.

When they actually did arrive, last November, Samuel was one of the first to get sick. Maybe it was the long voyage with no fresh food to eat. Or maybe it was the harsh winter that greeted them in the New World. Whatever the reasons, a number of colonists became ill during their first few months in Plymouth. Many of them died, Samuel included.

Somehow, the Billington family had been spared. Like the other survivors, they did their best to help the grieving families who had lost loved ones, all the while secretly feeling guilty that they had not been taken. Like the other survivors, they felt an inner resolve that the deaths of their fellow travelers— that the whole difficult journey—would not be in vain. Now John felt that determination all the more. If sickness had not taken his life, then by heaven no savage would take it either.

FOUR

CURIOUS

A MANUITT AND HIS COUSIN POTAK CAR-
ried the English boy until he woke up and
was able to walk for himself. Amanuitt had even
opened the pouch on his belt and given the boy
some of the No'Cake, parched corn which every
Nauset carried for energy during the hunt.

Potak and Amanuitt often hunted together. They
had a friendly competition over who was the better
hunter. Potak was taller than Amanuitt, more slen-
der and graceful. He could move silently through
the trees, slipping up on his prey without it ever
knowing he was there. Amanuitt, on the other hand,
understood the animal world better than any other
hunter in the village, including those more than
twice his age. He could read the signs left by an animal's wanderings. Even more, he could put himself
inside the head of the animal. By knowing how it
thought, he could hide in exactly the right spot and
wait patiently for his prey to come to him.

Up until today, Amanuitt and Potak were even in
their competition. With the discovery of the English
boy, however, Amanuitt had moved decisively into
the lead. Yet he hadn't been eager to bring his trophy

back to the village for anyone else to see.

"We should leave him here," he had said to Potak.

"To die?" said Potak. "We can't do that."

"It's not our fault he was out here wandering around by himself. It's his. If we just walk away, no one will ever know."

"We will know." Potak shook his head. "This is too important for you and me to decide. We have to bring the boy to the elders. They will know what should be done with him."

In the end Amanuitt gave in, but all the way along the trail to the village his mind seethed. This boy was trouble and nothing good would come from helping him.

*   *   *

The sun was low in the sky. The English boy was walking between Potak and Amanuitt. They had made good time in spite of the boy's inability to walk quickly, and were quite close to the summer village.

"You wait here," Amanuitt said to Potak. "I will go get the elders."

"There is no need," said Potak. "We can just take him into the village."

"But he is English. The elders may not want him to know the location of the village."

Amanuitt and Potak were so deep into their argument that they almost did not hear the noise behind them. They turned to find the English boy darting away to the left. Amanuitt and Potak cried out and gave chase.

They were not concerned that he would get away. The boy could barely run, and he made so much noise that one would have to be deaf to lose track of him. Besides, whether he ran to the left, right, or straight along the route they'd been on, he would be close to the village, which surrounded this last part of the path. The boy tripped and fell in the dirt. Before Amanuitt and Potak could reach him, everyone from the village had come out to see what was making all the noise. They all stood, looking down at the strange sight of an English boy, then up at the two Nauset boys who had delivered him into their midst.

*   *   *

"Tell me again how you came to find this boy," said Namanamoche, Amanuitt's uncle and the Sachem of the village. He was also like a father to Amanuitt. When Amanuitt's father and mother had perished in the Great Sickness, Namanamoche and his wife Weecum had taken in Amanuitt.

"He was in a clump of trees about three hours' walk west and north of here," replied Amanuitt.

"There was no one with him?" asked Namanamoche.

"He was alone. Do you think he was sent to spy on the People?"

"It is possible. Though I do not think it likely. Would a spy starve himself for days in the wilderness?"

Amanuitt stood silently facing Namanamoche. Namanamoche looked at him for a long moment.

"Potak says that if he had not stopped you, you would have shot the boy with your arrow. Is this true?" asked Namanamoche.

"I was taking no chances, Uncle." Amanuitt turned his eyes down toward the ground. "The English are tricky. It could have been a trap. I was ready to protect myself."

Namanamoche let another silence sink in.

"I understand how you feel about the English, my nephew. I, too, remember what they have done to our family. I, too, miss my beloved nephew Epenow."

"It's not just that." Amanuitt looked up into Namanamoche's eyes, pleading for understanding. "The English are devils. Their ways are strange and unnatural. They do not belong here. Why do they not stay in their own land with their own people?"

"Yes, some of the English have proven themselves to be bad men," Namanamoche agreed. "But others have been honorable and have treated us fairly."

"But how can we know which kind of English these new ones will be?"

"We cannot. We can only watch them and wait."

"It is wrong to trust them," repeated Amanuitt.

"Maybe so, Nephew. Time will tell. If the English attack us, then we will attack them in return. But for now we will be peaceful."

Amanuitt knew that this was the last his uncle would say on the issue. He bit his tongue to keep

from arguing any more and making Namanamoche angry with him. Taking a deep breath, he tried to make his voice calm.

"So what will be done with him?"

"For now we will show him hospitality. We will give him nourishment and shelter. In the meantime, messengers have been sent to tell Aspinet and the other Sachems of our people. They will come and together we will discuss this English boy and what should be done with him."

*   *   *

The English boy was placed inside an empty *wetu*. The wetu was the basic Nauset structure made from saplings and covered with mats of bark. Each family had one to provide shelter and to hold the family's possessions.

The boy was given venison and corn and cool, clear water. Amanuitt watched from a distance as the food and water were brought to the wetu and taken inside. His rage increased at the thought of an outsider enjoying the village's hospitality. Did the boy appreciate, or even recognize, the honor that was being shown to him? What had he done to deserve it?

Again Amanuitt wished that he and Potak had not rescued the boy. Yes, it would have been wrong to kill an unarmed stranger. But would it really have been so bad to leave him to fend for himself?

Amanuitt remembered looking into the boy's

eyes, the pain and fear he had seen there. There was only one other time in his life that Amanuitt could remember seeing such pain and fear in someone's eyes. That had been the last glimpse of his brother Epenow as the English ship sailed off, taking him away forever.

*   *   *

Amanuitt tried not to think about the English boy. He had chores to do and responsibilities to fulfill before it was time to sleep. There was wood to be chopped. Water to be fetched. But even as Amanuitt carried out his chores, his mind thought only of the English boy.

Soon it was time for sleep. Amanuitt wrapped himself in a deerskin and lay down on his mat on the sleeping platform of his aunt and uncle's wetu. But he could not sleep. He lay in the darkness, his mind replaying the scenes of the day over and over.

Finally Amanuitt got up and slipped outside, careful not to wake his aunt and uncle. There was a full moon that night and Amanuitt could see all of the village clearly outlined in the soft blue moonlight. He stood, letting his gaze sweep slowly from one end of the village to the other.

Each time his eyes would end up fixed on the same spot. The wetu that held the English boy.

Amanuitt studied the wetu, wondering about the boy inside. Was he sleeping? Or was he, too, awake and restless? What thoughts would be running through his head? Was he afraid? Did he miss his family?

Amanuitt found himself wandering over toward the wetu where the boy was sleeping. He wasn't sure what he expected to see there, but his feet seemed to have a mind of their own.

Slowly, he crept toward the wetu, all his senses tingling with awareness. He knew that his actions made no sense, that he should just go back to his own sleeping mat and crawl under his deerskins. Yet he eased himself to the dark opening in the wall that was the door to the boy's wetu.

Moving as slowly as if he were stalking a wild bird, Amanuitt eased his head inside. He scanned the dim interior of the wetu, looking for the English boy. Instead he found an empty straw mattress on the sleeping platform which ran along the inside of the wetu.

Before he could react, an arm snaked out of the darkness beside the open doorway and pulled him hard into the wetu.

Pressing into the tender flesh of his young neck, Amanuitt felt the sharp and unmistakable edge of a knife.

FIVE

CONNECTION

WHEN JOHN AWOKE IT WAS DARK AND he was alone. A sliver of moonlight filtered in through an opening above him, and his eyes adjusted to the small hut in which he found himself. He lay back on his mat and thought about his predicament.

He felt a wave of homesickness wash over him— for Plymouth Colony. This feeling surprised him. Until this moment he hadn't thought of Plymouth as home. In fact, he'd hated it with all his heart and wanted only to go back to England. Now Plymouth seemed like the most precious place on earth, and his troublesome family the most precious of people.

His thoughts were interrupted by a noise from outside the hut. John froze, his ears straining to catch anything. Another sound came, then another. He realized that they were coming closer. Someone was sneaking up on the hut!

John looked around for some place to hide. Nothing. He looked around for something to use as a weapon. Again, nothing. What was he going to do?

The folding knife!

John fished around in his pockets, praying that no one had searched him in his sleep. His hand closed on a smooth, hard shape. He pulled it out into the stream of moonlight. Yes, it was the knife!

He pulled the blade open and slid silently to the wall of the hut, beside the open doorway. Holding his breath, he kept himself perfectly still as a head slowly appeared in the doorway.

John waited as the rest of the intruder followed. He grabbed him from behind, holding the edge of the knife against his neck. The intruder was immediately motionless in John's hands.

John could feel this person's heart beating beneath his hands. He could also feel his own heart pounding in his throat.

What now?

Neither one moved for what seemed an impossibly long time. John's arms began to tire. How long could he keep this up? He closed his eyes for an instant, letting himself relax just a bit.

The intruder slammed backward into John, knocking him off his feet and slipping free. John scrambled back up in time to see the intruder spin to face him. It was the boy from the woods, the boy who had wanted to kill him, and he held a knife of his own.

John held his knife in front of him as the boy took a step toward him. The two boys circled each other in silence, each fiercely staring into the other's eyes. The boy stepped into the moonlight streaming through the smoke hole at the top of the hut, and John could see the anger and hate burning in his eyes. John felt like he was back in the woods, staring into those same eyes, waiting to be attacked.

John looked at the large hunting knife in the boy's hand. He looked down at the small folding knife in his own. There was, he realized slowly, no contest. John opened his hand and let his knife fall to the dirt floor. He held his hands up, palms open and facing the native boy.

The boy stared at John, confusion filling his face. He clenched his knife and lunged forward, almost stabbing John, but pulling back at the last moment. John stood completely still, unflinching, looking into the boy's face. The boy stared back at John.

After another long silence, the boy's arms dropped to his side. He turned his face away from John, stepping back out of the moonlight. John didn't move. Without looking at John, the boy turned and strode away.

John was alone again. Slowly, he let his hands fall to his side. He took a deep breath, suddenly feeling weak all over. He bent down and picked up his knife, closed it, and returned it to his pocket.

He sank down onto the mat. What had just happened? And what was he going to do about this strange, dangerous boy?

*   *   *

The next time John awoke it was light. He sat up and found a tray of food on the floor. Famished, he ate quickly. He finished everything except for a long piece of cooked venison which he left on the tray in

case this was all the food given to him that day.

John became aware of noise from outside. He went to the doorway and saw a group of men entering the village. For a wonderful moment he thought they might be his people who had come to rescue him, but a second glance showed that they were not.

John watched as the newcomers were welcomed into the village. Looking around, he saw that they were not the only new arrivals. The village was filling up with men in ornate dress. They wore bright bead necklaces around their necks and large feathers woven into their thick, dark hair. The newcomers carried themselves with confidence and pride. These were not ordinary men. John wondered why they were here. Could it possibly be because of him?

Out of the corner of his eye, John sensed someone watching him. He scanned the scene in front of him and found the native boy standing beside another bark hut across the village. The boy's eyes were looking directly at John. John looked at the boy for a moment, then stepped back from the open doorway.

Even though no one had made any kind of sign to John that he was a prisoner, he stayed inside. Like a caged animal, he paced back and forth across the bare floor of the hut. He found his thoughts turning again and again to his family back in Plymouth. What were they thinking right now? Had they given up hope for him? He wished that he could somehow get word to them that he was alive and safe.

But *was* he safe? He had been treated well so far, but what if the newcomers filling up the village had gathered to discuss his future? What if they were there to decide whether to let him live? Or not?

And what of the native boy who had twice been on the verge of killing John?

As if John's very thoughts had summoned him, the native boy appeared in the doorway of the hut. John stopped in his tracks and stared at the boy. Without thinking, he reached in his pocket for the knife. Catching himself, John pulled his hand back out and opened it so the boy could see that it was empty.

The boy looked at John as if John were the strange one, as if he couldn't figure John out. His face showed the same confused mixture of anger and sadness from the night before. Again, John felt his own feelings of sadness and fear. And again, he acted without thinking. He reached for the tray and the strip of venison.

John took a step toward the boy. The boy took a step back. John took another step forward, holding out the venison.

The boy looked down at the venison and up at John. Indecision played across his face. For a long moment he seemed not to know what to do. Slowly, uncertainly, he reached out his hand and accepted the venison from John.

The boy took a bite of the venison and chewed it solemnly. He handed the venison back to John. John took it, then bit into it himself. It was delicious. John held the venison back out to the boy, who accepted it and took another bite.

Between them, in perfect silence, the two boys ate the entire strip of meat.

John, deciding that he was closer to being the host in this strange situation, gestured for the boy to sit. The boy considered John's gesture, shrugged, and sat on the floor. John sat down across from him.

Now that they were seated, John didn't know what to do. There were so many things he wanted to say, such as: *Why are you so angry with me?* And: *Why did you bring me here instead of taking me home?* And most of all: *What is going to be done with me?*

With no way to ask his questions, John shrugged his shoulders in helplessness. Watching him, the boy mimicked his shrug as if he, too, felt the frustration of having no common language. Next to the fire pit at the center of the hut John saw a metal pot. Inside it was a long wooden stirring stick. Seeing the stick gave him an idea.

John took the stick and used it to draw a circle in the dirt. Inside the circle John drew two smaller circles for eyes and a line to represent a mouth. Below this face he drew a stick figure body sitting against a tree trunk. The Indian boy followed John's drawing with great interest.

Next, John drew a standing figure with a long arrow in its hand, pointing at the sitting figure. When he had finished, John pointed to the sitting figure and said, "John."

The boy looked at him, then down at the sitting figure John had drawn in the dirt. He pointed to the

drawing, then up to John.

"John," he said. John nodded happily. The Indian boy pointed to the figure with the arrow and then to himself. "Amanuitt," he said.

"Amanuitt," repeated John, suddenly feeling not quite so lost and alone.

SIX

HELP

A MANUITT KEPT HIMSELF BUSY TO DIS-
tract his mind from the English boy. There was
a lot to do. The first of the messengers Namanamoche
had sent out the night before were returning with the
elders from neighboring villages.

Amanuitt helped prepare the clearing for the
upcoming council. He swept the ground and fetched
water from the spring. As hard as he worked,
though, Amanuitt couldn't keep his thoughts from
returning again and again to the English boy. Once
when he was passing the wetu, he stopped beside
the door. He stood there for a while, struggling with
himself. Half of him wanted to go inside. The other
half said that was a crazy idea. While this debate
raged inside him, he was surprised by his Aunt
Weecum, the wife of Namanamoche and a powerful
elder of the village in her own right.

"Auntie," he stammered. "I will get back to my
chores now." He turned to go.

"Wait, Nephew," said Weecum. "Your uncle and
I have been talking. We agree that the best service
you could provide to the village right now is to watch
over our English visitor."

"I don't understand," said Amanuitt. "There is so much work to do to prepare for the council."

"And there are plenty of hands in the village to do that work. No, you can serve us all by keeping our young visitor company and making sure he is safe and comfortable."

Amanuitt reluctantly accepted his assignment. He didn't like it, but it was not his place to argue with the elders of the village. Slowly, he made his way to a hut across from the wetu that held the English boy. Amanuitt stalled there, watching the boy pace back and forth. Finally, he approached the wetu.

Amanuitt hadn't been surprised when the English boy first went for his knife, his laughable knife. But he *was* surprised when the boy had offered him food. And, if Amanuitt wasn't mistaken, he felt fairly certain that the English boy had surprised himself, too.

After the venison, when the English boy first began scratching in the dirt of the wetu's floor, Amanuitt had been confused. He'd studied the shapes the boy was making until all at once he recognized the scene from the day before.

"John," said the English boy, pointing to the drawing of himself

"Amanuitt," said Amanuitt, pointing to himself.

Once the boy had a name, Amanuitt had found himself wanting to know other things about him. As if reading Amanuitt's mind, John used his hand to smooth out the dirt to make another drawing. It was another version of himself, this time surrounded by three other figures: a man, a woman, and a boy.

"John's family!" thought Amanuitt. He looked at the figures in the dirt, strangely touched at the thought. He reached for the stick from John and drew a picture of his own family: mother, father, Amanuitt, and Epenow.

John nodded at the drawing, smiling at Amanuitt. Amanuitt took his hand and carefully erased the other three figures, leaving only himself alone in the dirt. John looked at him, confused for a moment. Then realization dawned on his face. He gave Amanuitt a look of surprised sympathy.

Amanuitt stood up, embarrassed by John's pity. He stood, feeling suddenly like an animal in a trap. Not looking at John, he turned and walked out the door.

The village was a bustle of activity. It took Amanuitt some time to locate Namanamoche.

"Uncle," said Amanuitt, grabbing Namanamoche's arm. "Please assign someone else to look after the English boy."

"What is the matter, Amanuitt?"

Amanuitt wasn't exactly sure how to answer that question. He only knew that he felt impossibly restless and he couldn't bear the idea of spending the rest of the day sitting inside a wetu—especially with a boy who suddenly knew more about Amanuitt than he had intended to share.

"We have many guests coming to the village," Amanuitt said finally. "There is much work that still needs to be done to prepare for them. Let me help with that. Don't make me go back inside. Please, Uncle."

Namanamoche studied his nephew for a moment before speaking. "All right, Amanuitt, you may help prepare for our guests."

"Thank you!" Amanuitt felt his spirits lift. "Who should I tell to go watch John—the English boy?"

"I have an idea," said Namanamoche. "The English boy is probably tired of being inside, as well. Take him with you as you work."

Amanuitt's spirits crashed. "You can't be serious, Uncle! What if he tries to escape?"

"For the present he is our guest, Amanuitt. Unless the council should decide differently, he is not a prisoner. Besides, I do not think he will try to run away."

Amanuitt stared at Namanamoche for a long moment, then shrugged his shoulders. Grown-ups!

* * *

Amanuitt carried water skins down the trail to the spring. John followed along behind. Amanuitt forced himself to go slowly. John limped along behind him, wincing slightly with each step inside his strange English moccasins.

The spring was a short distance from the village down a narrow path. It was one of Amanuitt's favorite places in the world, not because of the spring, but because of the large pond fed by it. This pond was the swimming hole for the village, and Amanuitt loved to swim. Not today, of course; there was too much to be done.

When they reached the end of the path, Amanuitt knelt before the spring and began to fill the skins with cool, clear water. John plopped onto the ground behind Amanuitt. With a groan, he pulled off his moccasins and rubbed his red and swollen feet. Amanuitt filled the last of the skins and sat next to John. He picked up one of the English moccasins and studied it.

John watched Amanuitt, curiosity visible on his face. Amanuitt turned the strange object over in his hands. It really was like no moccasin he had ever seen before. He put it next to his foot. John smiled and gave him a nod. Amanuitt forced it onto his foot, then stood and took a step. He gave a sharp cry of pain, sat back down, and yanked the horrible thing off his foot.

John burst into laughter as Amanuitt sat rubbing his pained foot. Amanuitt glared at him for a moment, then smiled ruefully. John held out his hand. Amanuitt handed him the moccasin. John stood and threw it off into the forest. He knelt, grabbed the other moccasin and threw it off into the woods, too.

Amanuitt clapped his hands and laughed. John joined in. The two boys laughed until their stomachs ached, relieved to have a common enemy, even if it was only a pair of shoes. Finally, they recovered their composure, picked up the filled water skins, and carried them back into the village. Amanuitt noticed that John actually walked better barefoot, and didn't seem to miss his English moccasins at all.

Back at the village John could not hide his curiosity as he studied the many distinguished men and women in their fine clothing. Amanuitt could see him struggling not to stare. For their part, the visitors did not seem startled to see a barefoot English boy in their midst. In addition to watching the visitors, John seemed fascinated by the village itself. Amanuitt saw John's interest and tried hard to serve as a guide, showing John different parts of the village.

Amanuitt took John into the wetu he shared with his aunt and uncle. It was larger and better decorated than the one John was using. John stared at the colorful bulrush mats that covered the walls. He touched the fine skins that covered the raised wooden platforms that served as beds. He seemed surprised to see an iron pot hanging over the fire pit in the center of the wetu.

"English?" John asked, pointing to the pot. Amanuitt nodded, yes. His uncle had traded with the English for many years during times of peace.

Next Amanuitt took John to the beach where a *mishoon*, or dugout canoe, was being made. None of the men were working at the moment; everyone was busy elsewhere preparing for the upcoming council. Amanuitt picked up a paddle and knelt in the unfinished mishoon to show John how a Nauset warrior and hunter paddled his canoe.

Finally, Amanuitt took John to the village gardens. The corn was almost up to the boys' knees, and the young bean plants and squash vines were lush and green. John seemed impressed and pointed to Amanuitt as if to ask if this was Amanuitt's garden. Amanuitt shook his head, no. He tried not to let himself be insulted by the question. How was John to know that only women and children tended the food garden?

It was getting late in the day, and Amanuitt was hot and tired. From the look of things, John was, too. Amanuitt knew they had to make one more trip with the water skins. But this trip, he decided, would have an extra element of fun. When they arrived at the spring, Amanuitt climbed up on a big rock and dove into the pond. The icy water felt luxurious on his hot skin. He swam down, down, down, touching the sandy bottom with his fingertips, then shooting back up to the surface.

He shook the water out of his face and looked around for John. The pond was empty. Amanuitt looked toward the path. There he found John standing completely still, his mouth hanging open. Amanuitt waved his arm at John, motioning for him to come in.

John just stood there staring uncomfortably. Amanuitt waved again more enthusiastically. Finally, John stepped up to the edge of the pond and began to tiptoe in ever so slowly. Amanuitt treaded water in the center of the pond as he watched John

gradually walk in until the water was up to his waist.

Amanuitt dove under the water and swam along the bottom toward John. When he could see John's legs, he burst up through the surface, splashing John. John shrieked in fear and yelled angrily at Amanuitt. Amanuitt rolled his eyes. What was this English boy's problem?

Amanuitt decided not to let John's attitude keep him from enjoying his swim. He scampered out of the pond and ran along the bank to the diving tree, a large elm alongside the pond that had a sturdy branch sticking out over the water. Amanuitt climbed up to the branch and walked out over the pond, balancing himself on the tree limb.

He looked down to find John staring up at him, his mouth hanging open again. Amanuitt bounced up and down on the branch, clowning for John's amusement. The branch swayed up and down beneath Amanuitt's feet until a loud *crack* sounded and the branch snapped in half like a flimsy little twig. Amanuitt felt himself falling like a rock.

In an instant everything went black.

SEVEN

RESCUE

JOHN WAS STARTLED WHEN AMANUITT dove into the pond. John was a city boy, or at least he had been until his father signed up the family for the *Mayflower* passage. Like most of the other English colonists, John could not swim to save his life. Water was for drinking, for fishing, and only occasionally, for bathing.

Amanuitt, however, treated the pond as if it were his home. John stared at the sight of his lean body slicing through the clear water like a knife through paper. Then he was gone. John couldn't see Amanuitt anywhere.

Suddenly Amanuitt shot up through the surface of the water and shouted at John, waving for him to join him in the water. John surprised himself by actually sticking a foot into the water. It was ice cold, and his first impulse was to turn around and walk away. But he didn't want to embarrass himself in front of Amanuitt, so he kept putting one foot in front of the other until he was in waist deep.

John looked around for Amanuitt, not seeing him anywhere. John shook his head in annoyance. A blast of cold water hit him in the face, and

Amanuitt's laugh filled his ears.

"Stop that!" John yelled. Amanuitt just laughed as he hurried out of the pond.

The next thing John knew, Amanuitt was above him bouncing on a tree branch until the branch cracked, dumping Amanuitt into the pond. On the way down, Amanuitt's head collided with the thick branch, and both disappeared under the surface.

John shouted, but Amanuitt did not come back up. The branch bobbed to the surface, but still Amanuitt was nowhere to be seen. John shouted louder, hoping to attract the attention of someone in the village. Still no Amanuitt. And nobody from the village, either. The pond was apparently too far away from the hustle and bustle in the village center. John couldn't hear them nor, he realized with growing desperation, could they hear him. The woods were deathly silent.

John knew he had to do something or Amanuitt would drown. He pushed his body forward into the pond. Flailing his arms, he tried to swim, getting a nose full of water in the process. His nose and throat burned, but he kept on. Harder and harder he pushed himself until his arm collided with something hard.

The branch.

John grabbed hold and pulled himself to the center of the pond. He looked down and saw a dark shape just below him. Pinching his nose with one hand, he pushed himself down with the other. His feet bumped something soft. John pushed harder against the branch above him. He let go of his nose and grabbed Amanuitt's hair with his free hand, water flooding into his mouth and nose.

John kicked his feet and pulled himself up to the surface, Amanuitt's hair still clutched tightly in his hand. Coughing and fighting for air, John grabbed Amanuitt's arm and pulled him to the surface. He grabbed hold of the branch again and pulled himself and Amanuitt toward the edge of the pond. Somehow he managed to drag Amanuitt out of the water and up onto the bank.

John dropped to his knees beside Amanuitt. He stared helplessly at the unmoving figure.

"Amanuitt!" John shouted. "Wake up. Please!" No response. He shouted again. Should he run for help? Just as he was about to, he decided to yell again, right next to Amanuitt's ear.

Amanuitt suddenly coughed, spitting water out of his mouth. John pulled him up into a sitting position and pounded on his back. Amanuitt gagged and gasped for air and then fell back onto the ground, quiet again.

John put his hand to Amanuitt's chest and felt it gently rise and fall, but Amanuitt's eyes were closed and his face slack.

"Help!" John shouted. "Please, someone— help!" No answer came. John thought again about running to the village to get help, but he didn't want to leave Amanuitt. That left only one thing to do.

John stood and bent down over Amanuitt. He grabbed under Amanuitt's arms and lifted his unmoving body up. John groaned with the weight, but somehow he managed to lift Amanuitt up over his shoulder and stagger forward toward the village.

Just when John thought he couldn't take another step, a tall shape loomed above him. He looked up to see the Indian boy who had been in the woods with Amanuitt the day before. The tall boy glared at John as if to say, what have you done to Amanuitt? Then the tall boy looked past John to the snapped branch over the pond, and a look of understanding altered his features slightly.

"Please help," said John, falling to his knees in exhaustion. The tall boy reached down and lifted Amanuitt off John's shoulders. He turned and headed down the trail to the village, leaving John to stare after him and pray that Amanuitt would be all right.

*   *   *

John spent the rest of the day alone in the hut. He tried to rest, but a confusion of feelings swirled through him. He found himself remembering a prayer he had heard one of the leaders of the Saints give shortly after the *Mayflower* landed. The man had thanked the Lord for sending the plague to kill the Indians. He had said it was God's plan to make room for the English to build their new colony.

At the time John had prayed along with everyone else. It hadn't seemed strange to him that a just and fair God would send a sickness to strike down one group of people to make room for another. But now, after meeting Amanuitt and his people, John wasn't so sure.

The Indian Plague hadn't seemed real to John before. Neither had the Indians who had died of it. Now, they were all too real. Especially Amanuitt.

Just before dark, an old native woman came to the hut. She was dressed in a long deerskin dress. Her face was kind but strong. She reminded John of his grandmother back in England. John felt a pang of sadness, knowing he would almost certainly never see her again.

"Amanuitt?" he said to the woman, hoping she would understand that he was asking about the boy's condition. She thought for a moment before putting her hands together and bringing them up to her shoulder. She laid her head against her hands and closed her eyes.

"He's sleeping," said John, deciphering her message. He laid his own head on his hands, copying her. Next, he moved his hands down by his side and made his body stiff.

She looked at him for a long while, pondering his question. Finally, she gave him a sad shrug as if to say, "I do not know if he will live or die."

* * *

John awoke to find two native men in the hut with him. Why were they here? he wondered. Did they think he had tried to kill Amanuitt? The men sat quietly, watching John. He nodded to them in a way he hoped would be seen as friendly. They did not respond.

There was a tray of food on the ground beside John's mat. He sat beside it and ate it in silence. Afterwards, he wandered over to the doorway of the hut. One of the men tensed as John approached the door.

"Sorry," said John.

The man did not respond. John stepped back from the door, giving the man a nervous smile. John looked out through the doorway. The village was completely filled with people. They were all dressed in colorful finery: feathers, animal skins, beads, shells. Many of them were old and carried themselves with dignity. Instinctively John knew that these men and women were the leaders of the Indians.

There seemed to be a lively debate in the clearing at the center of the village. John felt a shiver go down his spine at the thought that he was almost certainly the focus of the debate. He turned away from the door and walked back to his mat.

Time passed slowly. John tried everything he could think of to keep his mind off the dialogue going on outside. He even took the stirring stick from the cook pot and began drawing in the dirt. The two native men watched him but did not respond to his drawings in any way.

Just when John thought he would go crazy from the tension, there was a noise at the doorway. All three heads inside the hut turned at the same time to find the old woman framed within the open door. She stepped inside and spoke a few words to the men. They stood and walked past her, out of the hut.

John smiled at the woman, hoping that she had news for him. She smiled back. John's spirits soared. Before he could think of a way to ask her about Amanuitt, the two men reappeared in the doorway. Between them walked a figure on shaky legs.

"Amanuitt!" cried John happily.

"John," replied a weak but smiling Amanuitt.

John grasped Amanuitt's hand in his own. Both boys smiled at each other. With the woman's help, Amanuitt sat down on the mat opposite John. Amanuitt pointed a hand toward the cook pot. John picked up the stirring stick and handed it to Amanuitt. Amanuitt smoothed the dirt between them and began to draw.

First Amanuitt drew a stick figure with short hair. He pointed to the figure.

"John," he said.

John nodded, Amanuitt drew a number of other figures surrounding the first one. These figures had longer hair. He pointed to one of them.

"Amanuitt," he said.

John nodded again. Amanuitt pointed to the other figures, naming them in quick succession.

"Namanamoche, Weecum, Potak . . ."

John nodded and gestured around him as if taking in the entire village. Amanuitt nodded, yes.

Okay, thought John. *That's me here in this village.*

Amanuitt moved himself over a little bit and

began drawing another group of figures. These figures had short hair like the "John" figure. Beneath them Amanuitt sketched a long narrow box with a point at one end.

John was confused at first. He studied the drawing. Amanuitt added a few wavy lines beneath the boxy shape.

"A boat!" said John. "Men on a boat. A rescue party!"

Amanuitt responded to the excitement in John's voice by nodding his head vigorously and smiling. With one hand he pointed to the "John" figure and the Indian figures around it. With the other hand he pointed to the figures on the boat.

John watched, his breath frozen in his chest, as Amanuitt brought both his hands together.

*　　*　　*

All the rest of the day John could hardly contain his excitement. He pictured his family and how wonderful it would be to see them after such a long absence. Again and again he looked at the drawing Amanuitt had left in the dirt.

Outside, the village bustled with preparations for the upcoming meeting with the rescue party. John saw the boat in his mind, filled with brave colonists on their way to take him home. How good it would be to see all of them!

There was only one thing that darkened John's mood. At the head of the rescue party was sure to be

Captain Standish, the military leader of the colonists. As recently as the day before, the image of that fierce man of war coming to save him would have thrilled him.

Now all he could do was pray that Captain Standish did not attack his kind and generous hosts, and touch off a war that would devastate them all, English and Nauset alike.

EIGHT

REUNION

A MANUITT HAD AWAKENED FROM A DEEP sleep to find his aunt beside his bed.

"What happened to me?" he said, trying to sit up. His head filled with pain.

"Careful," said Weecum, gently easing Amanuitt back down.

A figure stepped forward into Amanuitt's field of vision. It was the *Powah*, the Nauset medicine man. He reached out a hand and felt Amanuitt's head.

"You struck your head against something hard," he said to Amanuitt. "I have seen people suffer much damage from such an injury. However, I think you were quite lucky. Your injury does not seem to have been too severe. Also, you were rescued by a quick-thinking young man."

"John!" said Amanuitt. He saw the confused expression on Weecum's face. "The English boy. His name is John." Then another question occurred to Amanuitt. "What about the council? Have they decided what to do about John?"

"There has been much debate, but no final decision yet. The great Sachem Aspinet has arrived with twenty of his closest advisors."

"Take me to them."

"You just rest now, Amanuitt. You have been severely injured and you need to take care of yourself."

"I can rest later," he begged her. "Please, Auntie. I need to be there." Weecum shook her head in exasperation, but she helped Amanuitt to his feet. With the help of a couple of men from the village, Amanuitt walked out of the wetu and over to the circle of elders who were meeting in the center of the village.

Amanuitt had never seen so many distinguished people gathered in one place before. Some of the faces he recognized. Others he had never seen before this day. One face stood out: Aspinet, the Sachem of all the Nausets. He held himself with a regal air, confident and patient.

Weecum helped Amanuitt find a seat in an outer ring of the circle. Several heads turned to observe this newest participant. Namanamoche politely interrupted the current speaker and drew everyone's attention to Amanuitt.

"This in my nephew," he said with pride in his voice. "It was he who discovered the English boy and brought him safely here to our village."

There was silence as everyone acknowledged Amanuitt, then the debate resumed.

"The English have become arrogant," said a man Amanuitt did not recognize. "They treat the forest as if it were their own. This boy is our opportunity to teach them a lesson."

Many members of the circle nodded their

agreement.

"He is but a boy," said a woman. "Think how you would feel if it were your son."

There was agreement with this, too.

Amanuitt's Aunt Weecum spoke up. "What's more, this boy helped Amanuitt. He showed great caring and compassion."

Amanuitt smiled, even though he was a little embarrassed at his foolishness.

But a man grumbled. "The English have shown us time and again that they cannot be trusted. It is time they learned that the People will fight back."

Amanuitt was surprised to recognize this latest statement as one *he* could have made just a day before. Now, it no longer seemed right to him.

"My brothers and sisters," Aspinet said in a strong, clear voice. "We have all heard much wisdom spoken in this circle. The English are indeed a challenge for us. In the future we may very well find ourselves at war with them. For now, however, we would be wise to make allies of them."

The circle considered Aspinet's words. One by one, each member acknowledged the righteousness of them.

"I have received news that bears on our decision," Aspinet continued. "A messenger has arrived with word from the English. They are heading down the seacoast in a boat, in search of their missing boy. I submit to you the only correct thing is for us to meet that boat and return their child to them."

The circle was silent, absorbing every word.

Amanuitt wanted to leave the circle and tell John the news. He decided instead to stay and listen to the rest of Aspinet's words.

"However," continued Aspinet, "I suggest we arrange for a show of strength to accompany the boy's return. Let us show the English that we will make strong friends. Let them also see that, if they ever choose to betray us, we will make strong enemies as well."

Everyone agreed with Aspinet's wisdom. But Amanuitt couldn't help but feel some fear at the thought of it. What if the Englishmen misunderstood the show of strength and took it to be a declaration of war?

Amanuitt hurried as best he could to John's wetu to tell him of the Englishmen coming for him.

He decided to keep his fears to himself.

* * *

The next day a great army of warriors was organized. Aspinet called for one hundred men to accompany him to unite John with his people. Amanuitt argued fiercely with his aunt and uncle for permission to go along.

"I have to go," insisted Amanuitt. "I was the one who found John. You said so yourself in front of the entire council."

"We almost lost you," said Weecum gently. "The Powah had to use all his skill and magic to heal you, but you have not yet completely recovered. You need to rest."

"I will be careful. Potak can come, too, and help me. I have to be there to say goodbye to John."

In the end, Weecum and Namanamoche relented. They were still worried for Amanuitt's health but recognized that his fate had become connected with the English boy's. They understood that Amanuitt had been at the beginning of the story and he needed to be there for the end, too.

That night Amanuitt stayed in the wetu with John. The two boys tried to sleep, but they were too excited. They built a fire in the pit and drew many pictures in the dirt. They shared as much as the language barrier would allow but felt great frustration at all the things they were not able to say.

*   *   *

The next day was very busy. The warriors prepared themselves carefully to accompany Aspinet to the meeting with the English rescue party. Bows were restrung and arrows checked for straightness and accuracy. Beads and shells were polished. Feathers were woven into strands of hair. No detail was overlooked.

Aspinet came to the wetu where John and Amanuitt were preparing themselves for their role in the upcoming meeting.

"Amanuitt," he said, "you have brought honor upon your village and upon all our people."

"Thank you, sir."

"And this must be our young English guest."

"His name is John."

"John," Aspinet repeated, startling John with the sound of his own name. He smiled at John before asking Amanuitt a question. "You speak the English tongue?"

"No, sir. I very much wish I did. There are many things I would like to ask John."

"Ah," said Aspinet. "I think I may have an answer for your wish." With that Aspinet turned and walked out of the wetu. John looked at Amanuitt questioningly. All Amanuitt could do was shrug, frustrated yet again by their inability to communicate, and his confusion over his uncle's words.

Aspinet returned with a native man Amanuitt had never seen before but who John seemed to recognize immediately. "Squanto!" yelled John with a smile. The native man embraced John enthusiastically.

"This is Tisquantum," Aspinet explained to the bewildered Amanuitt. "He is the messenger who brought us word of the English rescue party." Aspinet paused for a second. "He also knows how to speak the English tongue." A broad smile spread over Amanuitt's face.

With Tisquantum's help, Amanuitt and John were able to speak to each other for the first time.

"Thank you for saving my life," John said to Amanuitt.

"You are welcome," answered Amanuitt. "But I am ashamed that I came so close to attacking you as you sat there defenseless in the forest."

"Why were you so angry with me before you even knew me?"

Amanuitt answered John with the story of Epenow's kidnapping at the hands of the Englishman Hunt. As John heard the painful details, his face showed sadness, then anger.

"I am sorry, Amanuitt. Hunt is a very bad man and what he did was wrong. After that, I can understand why you would hate all Englishmen."

Amanuitt reached out his hand to John.

"Not all Englishmen," he said.

*   *   *

Soon it was time to go. The hundred men traveled side by side in two long columns with Aspinet at their head. John, with Amanuitt and Potak next to him, walked in the middle of the group. They were surrounded by the bravest warriors in the Nauset nation, dressed in their finest skins and armed with bows, arrows, and knives.

The group followed a well-worn path from Amanuitt's village down to the coastline. One of the men pointed up the coast. Amanuitt followed the direction of the man's hand and saw a small boat come into view. It held ten Englishmen. Amanuitt looked at John. John's eyes were moist with emotion. His body trembled. Amanuitt felt a wave of feeling come over him. He was excited for John. He was also sad for himself, knowing that he would miss his newfound friend.

Aspinet came over to John and Amanuitt and took them back from the beach and out of sight.

When the English boat came aground, a number of the Nauset warriors waded out into the waves and encircled it. The Englishmen were clearly nervous, looking around them at the great number of native men in their finery, their weapons in hand. The leader of the Englishmen, a tall man in the front of the boat, pointed his weapon at the warriors. The other Englishmen pointed their weapons. The warriors drew back their spears. On the shore, the archers drew back their bows.

John grabbed Tisquantum's arm and explained about the English leader, a man called Captain Standish. John said the Captain was quick to fight and did not trust the People. Tisquantum translated for Aspinet, who nodded his understanding. He asked Tisquantum to go quickly to the English and reassure them.

Tisquantum rushed onto the beach. At the sight of him, the English lowered their weapons. He spoke to them in the English tongue and they relaxed visibly. One Englishman in particular reacted to Tisquantum's words. Amanuitt studied this man's face, comparing it to John's. They looked very much alike. Amanuitt knew it had to be John's father.

Aspinet gestured to his men to gather around and prepare to take John onto the beach. As the Nauset warriors got into position, Amanuitt spoke quickly to Aspinet.

"Please, may I have a moment with him first?"

"Yes, but be quick."

Amanuitt reached into the pouch at his neck and took out his stone knife. He gave it to John who took it gratefully. John reached into his pants and took out a small object which he offered to Amanuitt. Amanuitt was not sure what it was.

Seeing Amanuitt's confusion, John pulled at one edge of the object and a blade swung out. John's knife! Amanuitt accepted the gift and held out his hand to John. John took Amanuitt's hand. The two boys looked at one another for a long moment, saying goodbye without words.

Aspinet wrapped a necklace of beads around John's neck, lifted him up onto his shoulders, and headed out for the boat. Fifty of the warriors came with him in a grand procession. The Englishmen helped John down from Aspinet's shoulders and into the boat.

From the beach, Amanuitt watched as John's father wrapped him up in his arms. John hugged the man back with great emotion.

Amanuitt wiped a tear from his own eye as John turned one last time and scanned the beach. Spying Amanuitt, he waved goodbye. Amanuitt returned the wave and watched as the boat slipped back into the sea with his friend.

Historical Postscript

In the Hands of the Enemy is based on actual events as recorded in the historical documents of the early Plymouth colonists. There was a real John Billington, Jr., and he was lost in the woods around Plymouth. He was rescued by the native peoples and handed over to a Pilgrim search party by the Nauset Sachem Aspinet and 100 Nauset warriors.

According to William Bradford's account, "One John Billington lost himself in the woods, and wandered up and down some five days, living on berries and what he could find. At length he light on an Indian plantation twenty miles south of this place, called on Manomet; they conveyed him further off, to Nauset." *In the Hands of the Enemy* condenses the action, having John discovered by two young Nauset men.

Sadly, years before that event, Thomas Hunt did kidnap 27 young Patuxet and Nauset men and sell them into slavery. Also, tragically, a great plague had decimated the populations of the New World in the early 1600s. On a happier note, there was a period of peace and cooperation between the English colonists and the native peoples that began in 1621 and lasted for many years.

To these historical events, fictional elements and characters have been added to construct the story. Aside from Aspinet and Tisquantum, all of the native characters are fictional; their names were taken from those of actual Wampanoag people as recorded in historical records.

While the terms "Saint" and "Stranger" were indeed used by the Plymouth colonists, historians disagree over the degree of animosity there was between the core religious group and the outsiders who joined them. Not enough firsthand information is available to know for sure. That's where the *fiction* of *historical fiction* comes in!

DATE DUE
